HOW MANY SNAILS?

a counting book

by **Paul Giganti, Jr.**

pictures by **Donald Crews**

A Mulberry Paperback Book
New York

Gouache paints were
used for the
full-color art.
The text type is Futura.

Printed in the United States of America.
10 9 8 7 6 5 4 3 2

The Library of Congress
has cataloged the Greenwillow
Books edition of *How Many Snails?*
as follows:
Giganti, Paul.
How many snails? / by Paul Giganti, Jr.;
pictures by Donald Crews.
p. cm.
Summary: A young child
takes walks to different places
and wonders about the amount
and variety of things
seen on the way.
ISBN 0-688-06369-1.
ISBN 0-688-06370-5 (lib. bdg.)
[1. Counting.]
I. Crews, Donald, ill.
II. Title.
PZ7. G364Ho 1988
[E]—dc19
87-26281 CIP AC

First Mulberry Edition, 1994.
ISBN 0-688-13639-7

For all
the people
who count

I went walking and I wondered:
How many clouds were there?
How many clouds were big and fluffy?
How many clouds were big
and fluffy and gray?

I went walking to the meadow
and I wondered:
How many flowers were there?
How many flowers were yellow?
How many flowers were yellow
with black centers?

I went walking to the lake
and I wondered:
How many fish were there?
How many fish were red?
How many fish were red
and had their mouths open?

I went walking to the garden
and I wondered:
How many snails were there?
How many snails had striped shells?
How many snails had striped shells
and stuck their heads out?

I went walking to the beach
and I wondered:
How many starfish were there?
How many starfish had five arms?
How many starfish had five arms
and were on rocks?

I went walking to the park
and I wondered:
How many dogs were there?
How many dogs were spotted?
How many dogs were spotted
and had their tongues out?

I went walking to the library
and I wondered:
How many books were there?
How many books were tiny?
How many books were tiny
and had numbers on them?

I went walking to the bakery
and I wondered:
How many cupcakes were there?
How many cupcakes had white icing?
How many cupcakes had white icing
and candy sprinkles?

I went walking to the toy store
and I wondered:
How many trucks were there?
How many trucks were fire trucks?
How many trucks were fire trucks
and had ladders on them?

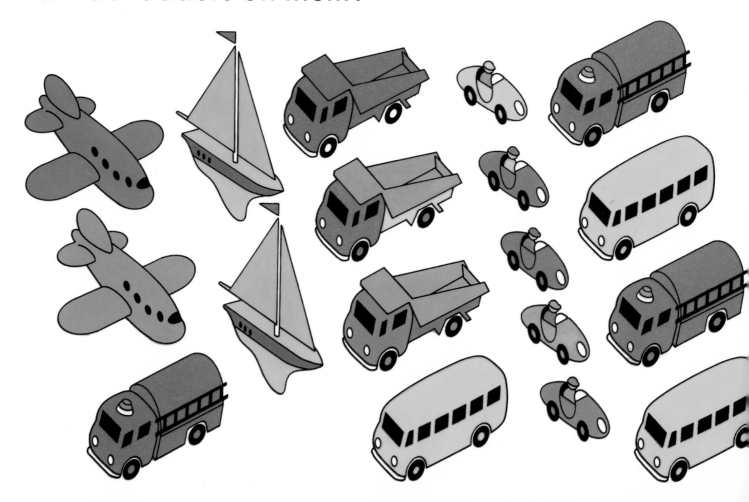

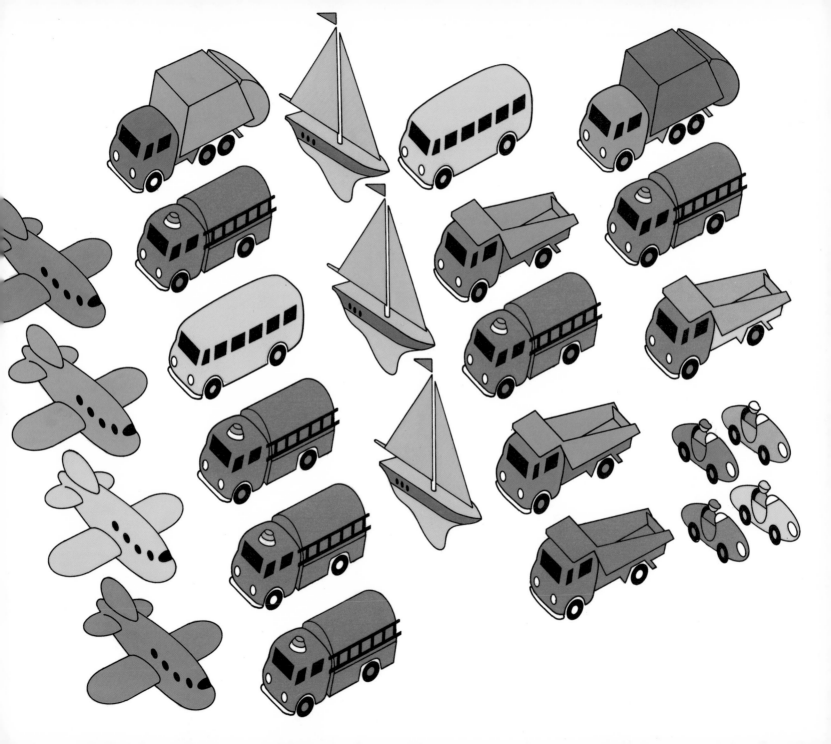

I went walking at night
and I wondered:
How many stars were there?
How many stars were bright?
How many bright stars
were shooting stars?

I went walking to my bedroom
but I didn't wonder
how many goodnight kisses
I would get.
Because I knew!